CLASSIC *Spirals*

FICTION

First edition published in 1976 by:
Hutchinson Education in association with the Inner London Education Authority Media Resource Centre

Reprinted in 1991 by:
Stanley Thornes (Publishers) Ltd
ISBN 0 7487 1005 1

Second edition published in 2001 by:
Nelson Thornes Ltd
Delta Place
27 Bath Road
CHELTENHAM
GL53 7TH
United Kingdom

01 02 03 04 05 / 10 9 8 7 6 5 4 3 2 1

A catalogue record for this book is available from the British Library

ISBN 0 7487 6437 2

Printed and bound in Great Britain by Martins the Printers

1

My friend Bob Wilson was always an odd sort of chap. Even when he was a kid he was a bit odd. Lots of people didn't get on with him. Poor old Bob. He didn't have many friends but I always liked him.

We went to the same school. It wasn't a bad place but Bob hated it. He was always getting into trouble. He kept doing stupid things. He wasn't really a fool but he kept doing stupid things. It's no wonder that he was always in trouble.

One day when Bob was about nine he climbed up a tree. There isn't anything odd about that, but wait and I'll tell you the rest. This tree was in the playground at school. We were told not to climb it. As a matter of fact we often did, but we were told not to

Bob got up to the top of the tree. He sat on a branch right at the top. I was half way up, when I saw the headmaster coming. Quick as a flash I started climbing down. I called out to Bob. 'Come on down!' I yelled 'Old Brown is coming.'

Bob didn't move. He just sat there at the top of the tree. 'Maybe he didn't hear me,' I thought. I yelled again. Bob still didn't move. I couldn't wait any longer. Mr. Brown was walking towards the tree. It's no good asking for trouble, so I jumped down and ran off.

I got away in time but Bob didn't. He was still sitting at the top of the tree when old Brown spotted him. Bob was in trouble again.

Later on I went to find Bob. I wanted to know why he hadn't got down the tree. He could have run away. I told him that Brown was coming. There was plenty of time to get away.

'Why didn't you run?' I said. 'Why didn't you come down?' Bob smiled at me. 'I was looking at the sky,' he said. I didn't know what to make of that. 'What do you mean?' I asked. He had a far away look on his face. 'The sky was beautiful,' he said. 'It was so blue. I just wanted to sit and look at it.'

Well, you see what I mean. Bob was a bit odd. Even when he was a kid he was a bit odd.

2

When Bob grew up he was just the same. I kept hoping that he would begin to act like a normal person. He didn't. As he got older he got more odd, more crazy.

Bob spent most of his time going from job to job. Sometimes he would stick at a job for a few weeks. Sometimes he left after a few days. No one can live like that for long. You have to get a proper job. You need money to live.

When Bob was very hard up I used to give him a bit of money. Not much. Just a few pounds to keep him going. I felt sorry for him. Bob wasn't like other people. He didn't fit in. He wasn't a layabout. Not really. He was a bit mad. He couldn't help it. He was born that way.

Anyway, Bob was my friend. I had to help him. He didn't have many friends. I was the only person he could go to when he was in trouble.

There was one thing that Bob really loved doing. He loved painting. I don't know much about painting. I was never any good at drawing or painting, but I could tell that Bob was good.

He did lots of paintings. He didn't ever sell them. He didn't make any money out of them. But they were good paintings. Bob put a lot of feeling into them. When I looked at those paintings I felt as if I could understand what was going on in Bob's mind. The paintings seemed to be part of him.

He always did paintings of places. Not real places. Just places he made up. Hills covered with trees. Fields of yellow corn. Yellow corn in the sunshine. Places like that. They were all in Bob's mind. He had never been to a place like that. He lived in the town and he didn't have the cash to go on holiday.

3

When I got married, Bob didn't come round to see me so often. My wife, Janet, didn't like him in the house. She thought that he was mad. Bob could tell that Janet didn't like him, so most of the time he kept away.

When I wanted to see him I went round to his flat. Well, I call it a flat, but it wasn't much of a place. He only had one room. It was a tiny little room and it was full of rubbish. There were tubes of paint all over the place. The walls were covered with paintings. The bed was never made and there were dirty cups and plates everywhere.

He spent most of his time in his room. He hardly ever went out. Some days he didn't bother to eat anything. Maybe he didn't have the money to buy food. He got very thin. His body was just a bag of bones.

When I went to see him I sometimes took some food. A few cakes. A loaf of bread. Things like that. He didn't always eat them. One day I took him half a dozen apples but he didn't eat them. He let them go bad.

'Why didn't you eat those apples?' I said. 'They are bad now. Why didn't you eat them?' Bob smiled at me. He said, 'Look, I want to show you something.' He dug about under the bed and got out a big bit of paper. When he turned it over I saw that there was a painting on it. A painting of the apples.

'I didn't eat the apples,' said Bob, 'I painted them. It took a long time and the apples went bad.'

I was feeling rather cross. Bob was a fool to waste good food. 'Of course they went bad,' I said. 'Apples don't last for ever.' 'Mine will,' said Bob.

For a minute I didn't know what he was talking about. Then I understood. He was talking about his painting. The apples in his painting.

What could I say to him? He was such a fool. 'That won't keep you alive. You can't eat a painting,' I said.

4

I've told you what Bob was like. I've told you a lot about him. I want you to see what kind of person he was. It may help you to understand what happened next.

You may not believe me when I tell you about it. It's an odd story. I don't understand it myself. I don't understand it, but I know it happened. I know it was real. I saw it with my own eyes.

I'm going on with the story too fast. I must tell you everything. It all started with Bob. I must tell you what he did next. Bob went mad. He was always a bit odd, but in the end he went mad. Crazy. Round the bend. I'll tell you how it happened.

Bob began to get all mixed up. He began to think he was another person. When people go round the bend they often forget who they are. It is part of the madness.

I once heard about a man who thought he was the King of France. He was a shop keeper but he thought he was the King of France. He kept giving people orders. In the end he was put away. Everyone could see that he was mad.

9

The same sort of thing happened to Bob. He forgot who he was. He thought he was someone else. He didn't think he was the King of France. No. Bob thought he was a chap called Van Gogh. A few years ago I saw a film about Van Gogh. I can tell you a bit about him.

Van Gogh was a painter. He was a real person but he died years ago. Van Gogh didn't have much of a life. He was very poor. He did lots of paintings but no one wanted to buy them. In the end Van Gogh went mad. He shot himself. When he was dead, his paintings began to sell like hot cakes.

That's who Bob thought he was. He thought he was Van Gogh. I don't know what put the idea into his head. I don't know why he thought he was Van Gogh, but he did. He believed it. He forgot his real name. He got cross if I called him Bob.

In some ways Bob was a bit like Van Gogh. He was a painter. He was poor. He was lonely. He was odd. Van Gogh was like that.

As I said, Van Gogh was crazy. He did one really crazy thing. Maybe you know about it? One day Van Gogh cut his ear off. He cut his own ear off.

No one knows why he did it. He had a row with his friend, then he went away and cut his ear off. He put the ear in a box and sent it to his friend. Poor old Van Gogh! He was a good painter but he was as mad as a hatter.

5

I told my wife about Bob. I didn't want to upset her because she was going to have a baby, but I had to tell someone about him. 'Bob thinks he is Van Gogh,' I said. Janet looked puzzled. 'Who is Van Gogh?' she asked. 'He was a painter,' I said. 'He died years ago.'

'Your friend Bob is mad,' Janet said. 'I always said he was crazy. He should be locked up.' I thought about that for a moment, then I said, 'Well, maybe Bob should see a doctor. I'll talk to him about it. I'll see if I can get him to go and see a doctor.'

That was what I planned to do. It didn't work out like that. Maybe I should have called a doctor there and then. It's easy to be wise afterwards. It's easy to be wise when you know what happened. At the time I thought I was doing the right thing.

I planned to go round to Bob's flat the next day. In the end I didn't have to, because he turned up at my place. Janet opened the door for him. She got a shock. She hadn't seen him for a long time and he looked different.

He had grown a beard and he was very thin. He looked as if he hadn't eaten a good dinner for years. His clothes were in rags and he was smoking a pipe. I had never seen him smoking a pipe.

There was a mad look in Bob's eyes. I thought that he might do something crazy, so I told Janet to go into the kitchen. She didn't mind going out of the room. She was glad to get away.

I took Bob into the living room. He sat down by the fire. 'Well Bob,' I said, 'it's nice to see you.' Bob stamped his foot on the floor. 'Don't call me Bob,' he said. 'My name is Van Gogh. Stop calling me Bob.'

I didn't want to upset him so I started talking about something else. 'Your beard looks good,' I said. 'When did you grow it?' Bob stared at me as if he didn't know what I was talking about. 'I've had a beard for years,' he said.

That was rubbish. I had seen him about a month ago. He didn't have a beard then. I remembered the film about Van Gogh. Van Gogh had a beard. Bob must have grown a beard because he wanted to look like Van Gogh.

Now I could understand why Bob was smoking a pipe.
Van Gogh often smoked a pipe. Bob's beard and his pipe
were part of the madness. He was trying to look like
Van Gogh. Poor Bob! He was really crazy.

I had to talk to him. I had to make him see that he
was ill. He couldn't go on like this. I put my hand
on his arm. 'Bob,' I said, 'you need to see a doctor.
I'll fix it up. I'll call the doctor.'

Bob pushed my arm away. 'I'm not ill,' he said. 'I
don't need a doctor.' He jumped out of the chair and
walked across the room. There was a picture on the
wall. Bob stood and looked at it for a moment.
Suddenly he grabbed it and smashed it on the floor.

'That picture is rubbish,' he said. 'I'll do a painting
for you. A good painting. How about that? How
would you like a painting by Van Gogh?'

I didn't know what to do. I had to make him
understand that he was ill. 'Listen to me,' I said.
'You are not Van Gogh. Van Gogh is dead. He shot
himself long ago. Your name is Bob Wilson. Van
Gogh is dead.'

Bob walked slowly towards me. I was afraid. I didn't know what he was going to do. He looked at me as if he hated me. 'You used to be my friend,' he said, 'but now you don't believe me. You think I am a fool.'

He got hold of my jacket. For a moment I thought he was going to hit me. 'I am Van Gogh,' he said. 'I'll show you that I am. I'll prove it to you. Just you wait and see. You'll be sorry that you didn't believe me. I'll make you believe me. You wait and see.'

I couldn't think of anything to say. Suddenly Bob let go of me. He ran to the door and opened it. 'You'll be sorry,' he said, then he ran out into the darkness. I went to the door but he had gone.

6

Bob had gone. I didn't know what to do. Maybe I should go after him, but what good would that do? I didn't know where he had gone. I sat down and thought about it.

I made up my mind to call a doctor the next day. That's what I would do. I would tell him about Bob. The doctor would sort it all out.

Well that was my plan, but it didn't work. I was too late. I didn't call the doctor in time. By the next day Bob was dead. Stone dead. He had shot himself.

I heard about it on the radio. When I got up the next morning I wanted to hear the news. I turned on the radio. That's when I found out about Bob. It was on the news.

A YOUNG MAN WAS FOUND DEAD IN HIS ROOM. HIS NAME WAS BOB WILSON. IT SEEMS THAT HE SHOT HIMSELF.

I heard the words but I couldn't take it in. I couldn't believe it. Bob was dead. I had been talking to him a few hours ago. Now he was dead. It was too late to call a doctor. Too late to save him. He was dead.

Janet was very upset about it. She started to cry. 'I wish I had been a bit nicer to him,' she said. I told her not to think about it. 'Don't upset yourself,' I said. 'You mustn't worry. You must think of the baby. No one can help Bob now.'

I couldn't go to work that day. I was too upset. I stayed at home and thought about Bob. Why did he shoot himself? Why did he do it?

Then I remembered Van Gogh. Van Gogh killed himself. He shot himself. Is that why Bob did it? The night before Bob died he said, 'I am Van Gogh. I'll prove it to you.' Maybe that's why he did it. Maybe he thought that I would believe him if he shot himself. Poor Bob! He was mad.

That evening I went out and got a newspaper. I thought there might be something in the paper about Bob. I wanted to know more about the way he died. I wanted to know who found his body.

There was nothing on the front page, but when I turned over I saw the words YOUNG PAINTER FOUND DEAD. There was a big bit about Bob. It said he was a young man with no job and no friends.

It was true. He didn't have any friends. I wasn't much of a friend. I let him down in the end. It didn't say how Bob got hold of a gun.

I was just going to put the paper down, when I saw something at the bottom of the page. Something that made me shiver.

It said: WHEN THE POLICE LOOKED AT THE BODY THEY FOUND THAT THE LEFT EAR WAS MISSING. IT HAD BEEN CUT OFF. THE POLICE LOOKED FOR THE MISSING EAR BUT THEY DID NOT FIND IT.

7

Two days later I was beginning to get over the shock.
I was still upset about Bob, but there was nothing I
could do now. Life must go on. I did my best to
forget about him.

It was all over. That's what I thought, but I was wrong.
It wasn't all over. It was only just beginning.

I was getting ready for work. Bob had been dead for
three days. Janet was in the kitchen getting my
breakfast. Suddenly there was a knock at the door.
'I'll go,' called Janet.

She went to the door and came back carrying a small
box. 'It was the postman,' she said. 'He gave me
this. It's for you.' I took the box and Janet ran
back to the kitchen. There were some eggs in the
frying pan. She had to keep an eye on them.

I took the box upstairs. I wanted to be alone when I
opened it. I had an odd feeling. Something told me
that Janet must not see what was inside. I went into
the bedroom and locked the door..

My legs felt like jelly, so I sat down on the bed. Slowly I began to undo the box. I didn't want to open it, but I had to. I had to look inside. My hands were shaking as I pulled at the string. My fingers seemed to get in the way.

At last the string was off. The paper was off. The box was sitting on the bed. All I had to do was lift the lid. I felt a bit sick. For a moment I thought that I couldn't do it, then I pulled myself together. Slowly I lifted the lid.

It was the ear. Bob's ear. It was lying there in the box. I just stood looking at it. It was pink and small. The cut side of the ear was smooth. It was not bleeding. It was Bob's ear.

I shut the box quickly. What could I do? I had to get rid of it. Janet must not see it.

Maybe I should tell the police. No. No, I couldn't do that. They wouldn't understand. They might think that I killed Bob. They might think that I cut his ear off.

I could tell them that Bob was trying to be like Van Gogh. No. They wouldn't believe me. Who would believe a story like that? I had to get rid of the ear. I couldn't tell anyone about it.

20

Just then Janet called to me. 'Hurry up!' she shouted. 'Your breakfast is ready.' I had to go downstairs. What could I do with the ear?

I went over to the window and looked out. A little way up the road I could see a large van. It was the dust cart. The dustmen were going in and out of the houses emptying the bins.

What luck! They would be at my house soon. I could put the ear into the dustbin. Soon it would be gone. Soon it would be hidden under tons of rubbish. Janet wouldn't see it. No one would see it.

Janet would want to know what was in the box. Of course she would. That was easy. I could tell her a little lie. I could keep the box and put something else in it. A new pair of socks. A tie. Something like that. I could tell her that my mother sent it. It was easy.

I walked quickly over to the bed. I picked up the box. My hands had stopped shaking. I had to take the ear out. I needed the empty box.

I lifted the lid. As soon as I saw the ear I began to feel ill again. I didn't want to hold it. I told myself not to be silly. I had to get it out of the box.

Slowly I put two fingers into the box and got hold of the ear. It felt smooth and warm. Yes it did. It felt warm. It should be cold and dead but it felt warm. As I held it in my fingers I got a shock. I thought it moved. I almost dropped it.

Maybe I was going mad. Maybe I would end up like Bob. Quickly I got a bit of paper and put it round the ear. The string from the box was on the floor. I picked it up and tied the paper carefully. The ear was well hidden. Now I could get rid of it.

I ran downstairs and went out to the dustbin. It wasn't empty yet but I could hear the dustmen just a little way up the road. Soon they would be here. I put the ear into the dustbin and ran indoors.

Janet was eating her breakfast 'Come on dear,' she said. 'Your eggs are getting cold.' I looked at the eggs. I felt sick. I couldn't eat anything. 'I haven't got time for breakfast,' I said. 'Sorry dear. I've got to dash off.'

As I went out of the house I saw the dustmen picking up our bin. Thank God. It was over. I had got rid of Bob's ear.

8

On my way home from work I stopped at a shop. I got a pair of black socks. I could put them into the empty box. Janet would never need to know about the ear. That was good. When your wife is going to have a baby you don't want anything to upset her.

As I walked up to the door of my house I stopped to look inside the dustbin. Yes, it was empty. The ear had gone. I went indoors.

There was a smell of cooking. Janet had made a big meal. 'You didn't have any breakfast,' she said, 'so I've made you a good dinner.' She was right. I was hungry. I hadn't eaten much in the last few days.

After dinner we sat down to see a film on the TV. Janet got out her knitting. She was making a little jacket for the baby.

As I sat there I felt happy. Everything was all right. Everything was O.K. The last few days seemed like a bad dream. Just a bad dream. Now I had woken up.

By ten o'clock Janet was looking very tired. She needed a lot of sleep these days. 'I think I'll go up to bed,' she said, 'I feel worn out.' I smiled at her. 'Go on then,' I said. 'Don't wait for me. I'll come up soon.'

Janet went off to bed. I stayed where I was. I didn't feel like sleeping. Not yet. It wasn't late. I wanted to sit in front of the TV a bit longer. It was Friday night. I didn't have to get up in the morning.

The TV was very loud. I turned it down a bit. I didn't want to keep Janet awake. I was just going back to my chair when I saw something. There was something under the table. It was moving.

'It's a mouse,' I thought. I was surprised. I had never seen any mice in the house. I went towards the table.

The mouse must have seen me coming. It ran between the table legs and went under a chair. I couldn't see it but I knew it must be there. It was no good trying to trap it but maybe I could chase it out of the house.

I got hold of the chair and lifted it up. Now I could see the mouse. For a moment it sat quite still on the carpet then it began to run. It was pink and smooth. It moved in an odd way. I stood looking at it. It wasn't a mouse. No it wasn't a mouse.

It was in front of my eyes but I couldn't believe it. I couldn't take it in. It wasn't a mouse. It was the ear — Bob's ear.

It was alive. It was moving. How could it move? What was it doing? How did it get out of the dustbin? My head was spinning. I couldn't believe it. What could I do? I had to get rid of it.

The ear was under the TV set now. It was going towards the kitchen. I ran after it. It was moving very fast. It seemed to be trying to get away from me. I had to catch it.

I ran to the kitchen, but the ear got away. It went into the hall. I followed it. For a moment I didn't know where it had gone. Then I saw it. There it was, in the corner of the hall. Now it was trapped. It was trapped in the corner.

Quickly I grabbed hold of it and picked it up. It jumped about in my hand. It was trying to push my fingers away. I didn't let go. I held on. My fingers were shaking, but I didn't let go.

I went to the back door. It wasn't easy to open the door with one hand but I did it. I went out into the garden. There was a full moon. The ear looked white in the moonlight.

At the end of the garden there was a pile of bricks. I planned to put up a shed one day. The bricks had been there a long time. I knew what I was going to do.

I put the ear on the ground and before it could move I put a brick on top of it. It was trapped. Quickly I took another brick and put it on top of the first one. I didn't stop. I went on until I had moved all the bricks. The ear was trapped under them. Now it couldn't get away.

I went indoors. My legs were weak and I felt sick. I had to rest. I had to lie down. I dragged myself up the stairs and got into bed. I don't remember what happened next. I must have passed out.

9

When I woke up, the sun was shining. I was lying in bed. I was still half asleep. It was Saturday morning. I didn't have to go to work.

Slowly I began to remember what had happened last night. I remembered about the ear. I couldn't believe it. It was crazy. It must have been a dream.

I got out of bed and went to the bathroom. The bathroom was at the back of the house. I could see the garden. I stood looking out of the window.

I could see the pile of bricks. Was the ear under that pile of bricks? Maybe I should go out and look. It was crazy. It must have been a dream, but maybe I should go and look.

I got dressed and went into the garden. I walked over to the pile of bricks. Slowly I began to move them. I lifted one, then I lifted another. Soon I got to the bottom of the pile. There was nothing underneath. Nothing at all. No ear. Nothing. It must have been a dream. Just a bad dream. I went indoors.

Janet was in the kitchen washing up. 'I saw you out in the garden,' she said. 'What were you doing?' I couldn't tell her so I said, 'Oh nothing much. I wanted some fresh air.'

Janet finished washing up and dried her hands. 'I must go out shopping,' she said, 'but I'll make a cup of tea before I go.' I needed a cup of tea. My mouth was very dry. 'Make one for me,' I said.

I went into the living room and Janet came in with the tea. She sat down beside me. 'I must hurry,' she said, 'I want to get the shopping done.' I smiled at her. 'Don't rush!' I said. 'There is plenty of time.' I looked at the clock.

The clock! I looked again. I could see something. It was small and pink. It was on top of the clock. I couldn't believe it but it was true. The ear was sitting on top of the clock. My hands began to shake. I dropped my cup of tea.

Janet hadn't seen it. She was picking up my cup. I grabbed hold of her arm and pushed her out of the room. 'Go into the kitchen!' I yelled. 'Go and get a wet cloth!' I wanted her to get out of the room. I didn't want her to see the ear.

She went. I shut the door behind her. Now what could I do? I had to think. I had to think quickly. I had to do something.

I looked at the clock. The ear was still there but it was moving. It was getting down. Suddenly it jumped. It hopped into the air and landed on the carpet. I ran towards it but I was too slow. I couldn't get it. It ran under a chair.

Janet came back. Before I could stop her she walked into the room. It was O.K. The ear was under a chair. She couldn't see it. Janet had a wet cloth in her hand. There was tea all over the carpet. She wanted to mop up the mess.

I grabbed the cloth 'Give me that!' I said. 'I'll wipe the carpet. I'll do it. You go out. Go and get the shopping. Go on. Hurry.'

Poor Janet! She didn't know why I was yelling at her. She went into the hall and put her coat on, then she ran out of the house I had upset her but I couldn't help it. Now I could catch the ear.

10

I looked at the floor. Where had the ear gone? Where was it? I walked round the room. I had to find it. I pushed the chairs out of the way. I moved the table. I pulled the cupboard away from the wall. I had to find it.

There was a rug by the fire. Suddenly I saw a little lump in the rug. It was moving. The ear must be under the rug.

Slowly I lifted one end of the rug. Yes, there it was. I had found it. I had to be quick or it would get away. I fell to the floor and grabbed it with both hands. I had caught it.

I sat up. Thank God. I had caught it. I found myself laughing. I was shaking with laughter. I sat there on the rug laughing like a madman. I couldn't stop myself. Soon tears were running down my face. I wasn't laughing. I was crying.

I had to pull myself together. I had to get rid of the ear. This time I had to make sure that it didn't come back again.

I put the ear into a box. When I had tied it up with string I put it into my pocket. Now I was ready to go. I went out of the house and got into my car. Quickly I drove off.

There were lots of cars on the road but I soon passed them all. I was driving fast. Every now and then I felt the box in my pocket. The ear was still there. It couldn't get out.

I kept driving until the town was far away, then I stopped. I got a map from the back of the car and looked at it. It wasn't far to the river. That was where I was going. I had it all worked out.

I started the car and went on. Soon I could see the river. It was shining in the sun. I was nearly there. I got out of the car and walked the last bit of the way.

The river was wide. The water looked green and still. It was very deep. I took the box from my pocket. The ear was moving about inside. Did it know what I was going to do? Did it have any feelings? No. I was being silly. It was just a dead man's ear.

I picked up a large stone and tied it to the box. Now it would sink. It would sink to the bottom of the river.

I held the box over the water, then I let go. There was a splash. For a few moments I could see the box, then it went down. Down into the weeds and mud. Down to the bottom of the river. It was gone.

The green water was smooth and still again.

11

When I got home Janet was waiting for me. She wanted to know where I had been. I couldn't tell her. 'Do you feel O.K.?' she asked.

I looked at my face in the mirror. I looked ill. My face was very white. 'I'm O.K.,' I said.

Janet came over and put her arms round me. 'You are upset about something,' she said. 'I can see you are upset. Please tell me about it. You can tell me.' I wanted to tell her but it was best to keep it to myself.

'I'm O.K.' I said. 'There is nothing the matter with me.' I went into the living room and sat down. Soon I got up again. I couldn't rest. I couldn't relax.

I went out into the garden. I had to do something. I couldn't sit about doing nothing. I needed something to do. I got a spade and began to dig.

My mind wasn't on the job. I wasn't thinking about the garden. I dug up most of the flowers, but I didn't care. I just kept digging.

The sun went down. It was beginning to get dark. The garden was in a mess and I was still digging. I had been out there for hours. I was so tired that I could hardly lift the spade. Still it had done me good. I was beginning to relax.

Just then Janet called me. 'Please come in,' she said. 'Stop digging now. It's dark. You can't see what you are doing.' I didn't want to stop just yet, so I called out, 'I won't be long. I'll come in soon.'

Janet wasn't happy about that. She called to me again. 'Please come in now. It's beginning to rain. You will get wet.' I looked up at the dark sky. It wasn't raining. The stars were shining. 'It isn't raining,' I yelled.

'Yes it is,' Janet shouted. 'It's just beginning. I can hear it tapping on the windows.' What was she talking about? It wasn't raining. I was standing in the garden and I could see it wasn't raining. What could Janet hear? What was tapping on the windows?

I dropped my spade and ran towards the house. I knew what it was. I knew. I ran round the outside of the house looking for it. I knew the ear had come back.

12

I found the ear outside the kitchen window. It was banging itself on the glass. It was trying to get in. How did it get out of the river? How did it get back? I tried to think but I couldn't.

I looked at the ear. It was wet and muddy. It was bleeding. There was blood on the window. There were drops of blood on the window sill.

I put my hands over my eyes. What could I do now? I had done my best to get rid of the ear but it had come back. Maybe I would never get rid of it. Maybe it would follow me about for ever. I couldn't stand it any more. I would go mad.

I grabbed hold of the ear. It was hurt. Badly hurt. Blood was running down my hand. Maybe I could kill it. Maybe I could finish it off.

I ran to the end of the garden. My spade was lying on the ground. I picked it up. The ear was wet with blood. It was slippery. It slipped out of my hand and lay there on the ground.

For a moment I stood and looked at it. This time it wouldn't get away. This time I would get rid of it. I would kill it.

I lifted the spade above my head. The ear began to move, then I hit it. I hit it as hard as I could. The spade crashed down on top of it. Then I hit it again. I didn't stop. I just kept hitting it.

My head was spinning. I didn't know what I was doing. I hit the ear again and again. I hated it. I had to kill it. Nothing else mattered. I had to kill the ear.

At last I stopped. I couldn't lift the spade again. I was weak. My arms were shaking. The spade fell from my hand.

I looked at the ear. It was a mess. Just blood and skin. Not an ear. Not any more. Just blood and skin. Just a dead thing. It made me feel sick.

Janet called to me again. I had to go in. I looked at the dead ear. I was going to leave it there. I was going to leave it lying on the ground, then I thought, 'No. I must move it. I must hide it.'

I didn't want to pick it up, but I had to. I put my handkerchief over the thing, then I picked it up. Just then I saw Janet coming towards me. It was too late to hide the ear. In a moment she would see it. Quickly I put it into my pocket.

Janet came running across the garden. She was smiling. It was O.K. She hadn't seen the ear. She got hold of my arm. 'Come on,' she said. 'You are tired. You have been digging for hours. Come indoors with me.' She held my arm and pulled me into the house. 'Sit down by the fire,' she said, 'and I'll make you a cup of tea.'

Janet went out to the kitchen. I sat there by the fire. The dead ear was in my pocket. I couldn't leave it there. It was bleeding. Soon I would have blood all over my jacket. Janet would see it. Where could I put the ear? Where could I put it?

There was a cupboard in the room. That would do. I could hide it in there for the night. I could lock the cupboard door. Tomorrow I could take the ear out and burn it. I could burn what was left of it.

Quickly I put the ear into the cupboard. I locked it and put the key in my pocket. Janet came back with my cup of tea. She sat down beside me. 'I hope you are feeling O.K.,' she said. 'I don't want to go away if you are feeling ill.'

'What are you talking about?' I asked. 'You aren't going away.' Janet smiled. 'Don't tell me that you have forgotten. I'm going to stay with my mother for a few days. I told you about it weeks ago. You said it would be good for me.'

Yes. It was true. I had forgotten all about it. Janet had planned to go over to her mother's house. Now I remembered. What luck! She was going away tomorrow. I would be by myself. I would have plenty of time to get rid of the dead ear.

I went up to bed feeling tired but happy.

13

In the morning I woke up with a jump. I could hear something. A banging noise. It was coming from downstairs. There must be someone at the door.

Janet was still asleep. I didn't wake her. I slipped out of bed and went downstairs. When I got to the hall the banging noise was louder. It wasn't coming from the door. No. It was coming from the living room.

Slowly I opened the living room door. The noise was coming from the cupboard. It couldn't be true. It couldn't be. The ear was dead. I killed it. But something was banging about in the cupboard. It must be the ear.

I ran out of the living room and went to the kitchen. I put the radio on. I turned it up, so that it was very loud. I didn't want Janet to hear the banging.

Soon she came downstairs. She was carrying her case. That was good. She was ready to go. 'Hurry up!' I said. 'You don't want to miss the train.'

Janet had breakfast in the kitchen, then I got her out of the house at top speed. I drove her to the station and saw her get on to the train. After that I went home. At last I was alone with the ear.

14

As soon as I stepped inside the house I could hear the banging noise. I went into the living room. The cupboard door was locked but it was shaking. The wood was beginning to crack open. I went cold all over.

I took the key from my pocket and put it in the lock. I had to open that cupboard and look inside. I needed to see the ear. Why wasn't it dead? What had happened to it?

Slowly I opened the door. I thought I would see a mess of blood and skin — but no. I got a shock. The ear was pink and smooth. It wasn't bleeding. It wasn't even hurt. Not at all. Somehow it had put itself together again. Somehow it had come back to life.

Quickly I shut the cupboard door. Now I had to face the truth. I couldn't fool myself any longer. *I couldn't get rid of the ear.* Whatever I did it would come back. I couldn't stop it. I couldn't even kill it. There was nothing more I could do. Nothing at all.

I sat down on the floor and put my hands over my face. Why did this happen to me? Why me? What did the ear want? What was it trying to do? It was Bob's ear. What had happened to it?

I began to think about Bob. I had been thinking about the ear for days. I had almost forgotten about Bob. What did Bob say the last time I saw him? What did he say? Yes. I remembered. He said, 'I am Van Gogh. I'll prove it to you. You'll be sorry that you didn't believe me.' That's what he said.

What did Bob mean? How could he be Van Gogh? Bob didn't know what he was saying. He was off his head. He was mad. Or was he? I sat on the floor thinking hard. What if Bob wasn't mad? What if it was true?

Suddenly I jumped up. I had an idea. I needed to find out a bit more about Van Gogh. I checked the cupboard door. It was cracking but it would hold on for a bit longer. I put a chair against it then I dashed out of the house.

I got into my car and drove off to the shops. I went to five bookshops. In the end I found what I was looking for. It was a book called THE LIFE OF VAN

GOGH. I paid for the book and drove home as fast as I could. The ear was still safe in the cupboard.

I wanted to know what happened to Van Gogh. He shot himself but where did they put his body? Where was his grave? I turned the pages of the book.

It was all there. Everything I wanted to know. Van Gogh died in France. He was buried in a small town not very far from Paris. There was even a photo of his grave.

I shut the book with a bang. I knew what I was going to do. Maybe there was a way to get rid of the ear. It was crazy but maybe it would work. It would cost me a lot of money but I had to try it.

I didn't mess about. I booked a seat on a 'plane to France. I had to be at the airport in two hours or I would miss the 'plane. I had to hurry. Quickly I put the ear into a box. When it was safe in my pocket, I set off.

It was a rush but I made it. I got to the airport a few minutes before the 'plane left. Soon I was on my way to France. No one could see the small box in my pocket. The ear was very still and quiet.

15

The 'plane landed at Paris. I left the airport as fast I could and got a taxi. The taxi driver was French. He didn't understand me. I couldn't tell him where I wanted to go.

For a moment I didn't know what to do. How could I make him understand? Then I thought of a way. It was easy. I showed him my book about Van Gogh.

I turned the pages until I came to the photo of the grave. The driver understood. He nodded his head. I jumped into the taxi and I was on my way.

I sat in the taxi for hours. I didn't know it was so far. I began to worry. Maybe I shouldn't have come. It was a crazy idea. Crazy.

Of course it was crazy, but everything else was crazy too. Bob − the ear − Van Gogh − it was all crazy. It was crazy but it was real. The ear in my pocket was real. I couldn't just forget about it. That wouldn't make it go away. I had to go on. I couldn't give up now.

I looked out of the taxi window. I could see a field.
It was full of yellow corn. Yellow corn in the sunshine.
I had the feeling that I had been here before. That
was silly. I had never been to France.

I kept looking. Yes, I had seen it before. Where was
it? Where had I seen this field before? Suddenly I
remembered. In one of Bob's paintings. That was it.
That's where I had seen it.

As the taxi drove on I kept seeing places that I knew.
Places that Bob had painted. How did Bob do it?
How did he paint these places? He had never been to
France. You can't do a painting of a place you have
never seen.

I was still thinking about it when the taxi stopped. I
was there. I was there at last. Van Gogh's grave. I
had made it. The taxi drove off and I was left alone.
There was no one about. Just me.

Slowly I walked towards the grave. I took the box
from my pocket and opened it. The ear wasn't moving.
It was lying very still. I lifted it out and held it in
my hand. It seemed very small and helpless. Just a
small pink ear.

Suddenly I felt sorry for it. It had made my life hell, but I felt sorry for it. Was it dead or was it alive? I didn't know. Maybe it had feelings. Maybe it could hear me. I put the ear close to my face and talked to it.

'I don't know where you belong,' I said. 'I don't know who you belong to. Maybe you are Bob's ear. Maybe you are Van Gogh's ear. I don't know what to think.' The ear didn't move. It lay there in my hand. I had a feeling that it could hear me.

'I'm going to leave you here with Van Gogh,' I said. 'I'm going to put you in his grave. I think you belong here.'

I stood by the grave for a moment. The sun shone down on me. Everything was very still and quiet. I could hear the birds singing. I didn't understand what had happened. Bob. . . Van Gogh. . . the ear. . . I didn't understand it at all. Now it didn't seem to matter. There are so many things that no one understands.

I had one more thing to do. I had to bury the ear. I dug a small hole on top of the grave. The ear didn't try to get away. It didn't move. It felt cold in my hand. Cold and dead. I put it into the grave and covered it over.

It was done. There was nothing more I could do. I turned and began to walk away, then I stopped. There were some yellow flowers growing by a wall. Big yellow flowers. I picked one and went back. Slowly I put it on top of the grave.

'Please don't follow me,' I said to the ear. 'This is where you belong.' Then I started walking. I had a long way to go.

The Spirals Series

Fiction

Jim Alderson
The Witch Princess

Jan Carew
Death Comes to the Circus
Footprints in the Sand
Voices in the Dark

Barbara Catchpole
Laura Called
Nick

Susan Duberley
The Ring

Keith Fletcher and Susan Duberley
Nightmare Lake

John Goodwin
Dead-end Job
Ghost Train

Angela Griffiths
Diary of a Wild Thing

Marian Iseard
Loved to Death

Anita Jackson
The Actor
The Austin Seven
Bennet Manor
Dreams
The Ear
A Game of Life and Death
No Rent to Pay

Paul Jennings
Eye of Evil
Maggot

Helen Lowerson
The Biz

Margaret Loxton
The Dark Shadow

Patrick Nobes
Ghost Writer

David Orme
City of the Roborgs
The Haunted Asteroids

Kevin Philbin
Summer of the Werewolf

Bill Ridgway
Jack's Video
Mr Punch

Julie Taylor
Spiders

John Townsend
Back on the Prowl
Beware the Morris Minor
Fame and Fortune
Night Beast
A Minute to Kill
Snow Beast

Non-fiction

Jim Alderson
Crash in the Jungle

David Orme
Hackers

Bill Ridgway
Lost in Alaska

Julie Taylor
Lucky Dip

John Townsend
Burke and Hare: The Body Snatchers
SOS

Plays

Jan Carew
Computer Killer
No Entry

Julia Donaldson
Books and Crooks

John Godfrey
When I Count to Three

Angela Griffiths
Wally and Co

Paul Groves
Tell Me Where it Hurts

Barbara Mitchelhill
Punchlines
The Ramsbottoms at Home

Bill Ridgway
Monkey Business

John Townsend
A Bit of a Shambles
Breaking the Ice
Cheer and Groan
Clogging the Works
Cowboys, Jelly and Custard
Hanging by a Fred
Hiccups and Slip-ups
Jumping the Gun
The Lighthouse Keeper's Secret
A Lot of Old Codswallop
Making a Splash
Over and Out
Rocking the Boat
Spilling the Beans
Taking the Plunge

David Walke
The Good, the Bad and the Bungle
Package Holiday